The Melodious Habits
of Wiggle McFiggle

Charleston, SC
www.PalmettoPublishing.com

The Melodious Habits of Wiggle McFiggle

Copyright © 2021 by Darryl Washington, D.Ed.

All rights reserved.

First Edition

Paperback ISBN: 978-1-64990-782-0
Hardcover ISBN: 978-1-64990-781-3
eBook ISBN: 978-1-64990-783-7

The Melodious Habits
of Wiggle McFiggle

Darryl Washington D.Ed.

Author's Note

When I was a little boy, I had a habit of singing for no particular reason, but as I sang life always seemed good. I felt like a cup that was overflowing as if I would spill over, my happiness was more than enough!

Life, at its fullest, is melodious and flows like an unending song in your heart day-after-day. But to stay in the rhythm of it, we must know the words and the meaning within the song. If you understand the melody of life, it sets the tone and direction of every day and causes you to be joyful. So much so, you will affect those that you encounter every day, helping them also to live a melodious life. Every boy and girl must know the melodious life, so that everyone can live in a more beautiful world.

Eventually, I discovered the words of my song came from heaven, and as long as I stayed in tune with it my life was full. Life is a gift from God, one that we should cherish and thank Him for it at all times.

My wish is that every boy and girl would have this song from heaven and to develop the melodious habit of thanking the One who so willingly gave this glorious gift.

In His Love, for His love for you---Dr. Darryl Washington

In the humble, sweet town called Pleasant Collet,
lived Wiggle McFiggle who blessed all who he met.
Wiggle brought joy and happiness to every corner and bend,
He blessed all that he met, both stranger and friend.
Marvelous was his way in bringing an ease in his flow,
A greeting, kind gesture, and kindness he'd show.

Psalm 98:1 NIV
Sing to the LORD a new song, for he has done marvelous things;

I

Wiggle McFiggle maintained a habit of praying all day long,
Keeping him joyful in speaking to God, humming,
and singing a constant love song.
Wiggle would sing unto the Lord a perfectly sweet
and melodious cord,
Rejoicing in His goodness overflowed from his heart
and continually poured.

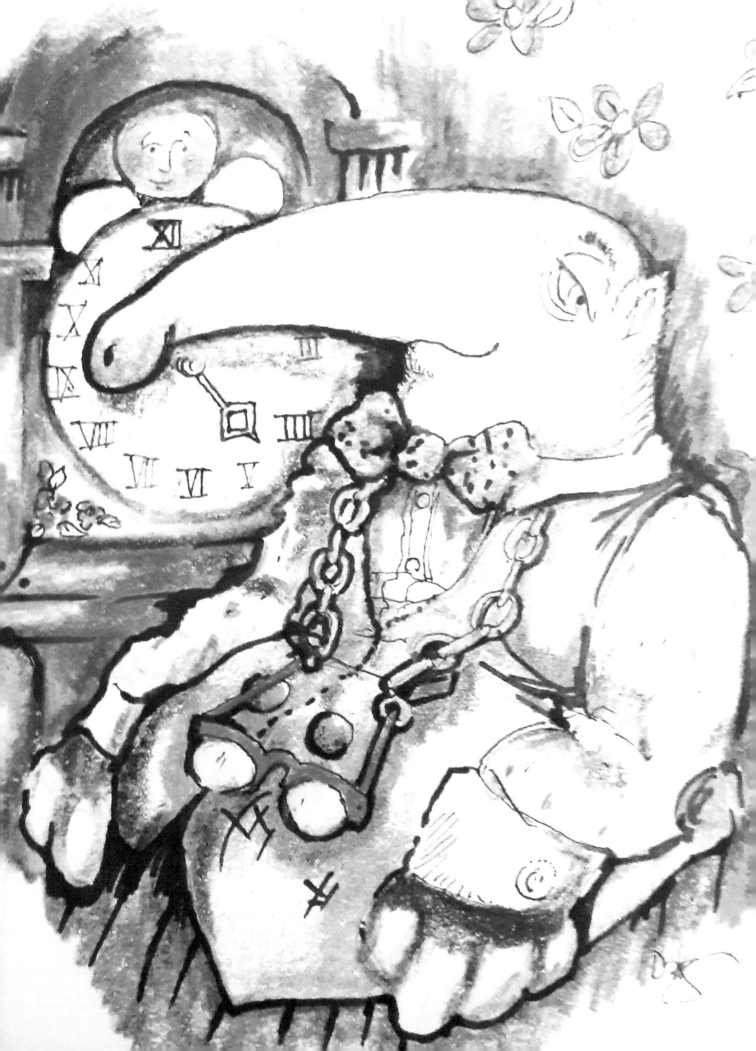

Wiggle was a stout fellow, with a prominent snout,
shaped like a flute for a musical sound to come out.
Always adorned with a colorful bowtie,
a vibrant vest to attract all passersby.
Around his neck he wore a brilliant gold chain,
Attaching his spectacles to ensure they always remained.

He lived in a nook, in a bright-colored house,
In his tree hung a matching smaller birdhouse.
He was a platemaker by trade,
The finest of wares in a storefront on parade.
He fastidiously decorated his stylish plates,
After he finished them, they would go in to bake.

Psalm 46:10, NIV
"Be still, and know that I am God."
If you are not still, you will not know that God is God.

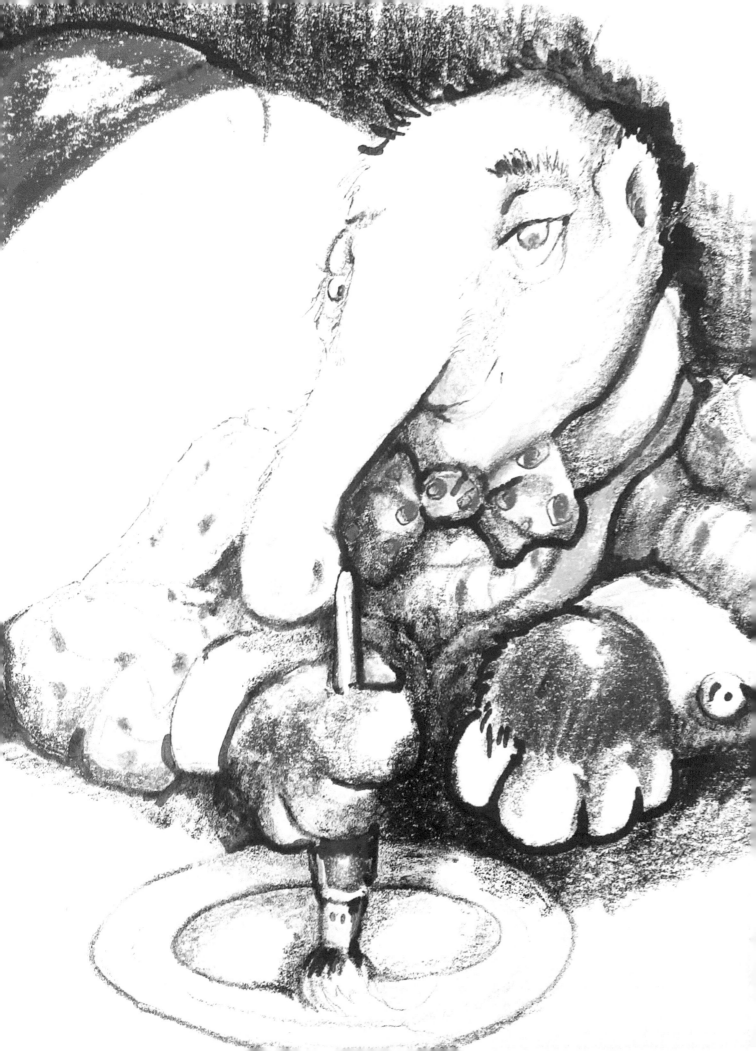

Wiggle McFiggle had growing success,
but it left him busied and hurried some days with no rest,
therefore, sadly he could no longer do his very best.
He worked harder and harder at the plates he did make,
So many! So many! He aspired to create!

Psalm 46:10 NIV
He says, "Be still, and know that I am God;

An unfortunate revelation with all this hurried up work,
He forgot his good deeds, lost his vigor and perk.
His habit to pray had begun to dwindle away,
which he no longer continued day after day.
He forgot how amazed, by fixing his gaze,
On his Lord, he once praised.

Psalm 62: 5 NLT
Let all that I am wait quietly before God, for my hope is in Him.

Awakened one morning,
cold wind blew through his window chilly air,
Wiggle barreled out of his bed, washed his face,
and fussed at his hair,
Then to make his way to keep track of time,
He hastened to his breakfast quickly to dine.

Psalm 119:147 NIV
I rise before dawn and cry for help; I have put my hope in your word.

Glurp! Glurp! Glurp! Glurp!
His breakfast went down his gullet in a swirl,
Not a minute to waste in his hurried-up world.
Stomp, stomp, stomp, stomp, off he dashed not looking about,
Maintaining his course to get on his route!

Psalm 35:15 NIV
My times are in your hands; deliver me from the hands of my enemies,
from those who pursue me.

The noises that were made such as a squeak,
click, clack, flop, and a flip,
were the many sounds that were made by Wiggle's neighbors
as they peeped out their windows, shutters, and doors,
expecting to hear his praise to unto the Lord
everyone knew how much he adores.

Psalm 115:17 NIV
It is not the dead who praise the LORD,
those who go down to the place of silence;

Disappointed they were to hear not a hoot,
his countenance sad, and no sound,
not a peep from his melodious snoot.
They expected each day as he left from his house,
To be uplifted by his praise-filled words that provoked joy
in their hearts with a rouse.
He would bellow a magnificent and glorious shout,
Hallelujah to God that was heard all about!

His neighbors and friends then went on their way,
In their usual, frown-faced, and grisly dismay,
Now they were saddened about their friend's turnabout.
how they missed those fine days as Wiggle came out.

Wiggle McFiggle began to change his neighbors and friends,
Their attitudes did sway, as they began to bend.
They missed the encouragement that reminded them to stay,
full of love, care, and kindness throughout the whole day!

Psalms 30:5 KJV
…in his (God's) favour is life: weeping may endure for a night,
but joy cometh in the morning.

Wiggle McFiggle, flew to his work,
Striving to finish all his plates in a spurt.
Mr. McDread was Wiggles' mean, haughty boss,
Who saw Wiggle break a plate and, in the trash, he did toss,
A plate he had minted, painted, and glossed.

Psalm 109:1-20 ESV
Be not silent, O God of my praise!
For wicked and deceitful mouths are opened against me…

Mr. McDread shouted, Oh! The profit we lost!
Fuming in red, was Mr. McDread,
Spewing his grief, through his yellow clenched teeth!
Do it again and I will have no more need,
For you, Mr. McFiggle, for this insidious deed!

At this rebuke, Wiggle fell in a stoop,
he froze like a stump, with his throat in a lump.
Wiggle shouted aloud with a heavy heart,
I will make no more plates; I will have no more part!

Just at that time, the lunch whistle blew,
Then off did he go with the rest of the crew.
He sulked and felt glum for his tenderly heart was just rent,
By the despicable words that his boss just did vent.

Be seated at his table was Bella Believe,
Smacking her bill, she rolled up her sleeves and sipped of her tea.
Chip, chip, chip, chomp, chomp, splick, splick,
she hacked at her lunch,
She ate at her salad, a colorful bunch.
She was about to chomp down on her food in the round,
But turning around at a boisterous sound
Wiggle! My friend stop that bemoaning right now!

Psalm 27:1 TPT
The Lord is my revelation-light to guide me along the way;
he's the source of my salvation to defend me every day. I fear no one!
I'll never turn back and run from you, Lord; surround and protect me.

I am sorry Miss Bella as tears dropped on his sleeve,
Things are in such a bust; you understand, I do trust.
Nothing seems bright, nor anything right.
Oh, precious dear one, so sweetly she did say,
Encouragement is near, remember trust and obey!

Psalm 118:13- NIV
I was pushed back and about to fall, but the Lord helped me.

Consider these words I heard from these birds.
A tweet and some toots they sputtered out loot.
I captured the wisdom from God that was bidden,
Like you my heart was weighed to the ground,
But at their words, I did rebound.
From the glorious words of these, oh these God-loving birds!

Psalms 90:12-KJV
"So teach us to number our days, that we may apply our hearts unto wisdom."

The word of our Lord is ever recorded,
I listed and gleaned as they had reported.
Have you no don't, God has planned it all out,
our feathers and wings and the way that we sing!
In the air way up high, we are given to fly.

Psalm 37:4-5 NIV
"Take delight in the Lord, and he will give you the desires of your heart."

We are created by God and us not our self,
All worries and cares should stay on the shelf,
Built like a house, we have nothing left out,
We can ask all we can for Him to remember His plan.
Thank God for His light to make everything right,
and all things seem bright!

Suddenly, Wiggle remembered the joy in God that he knew,
He praised, talked, and sang and his strength did renew.
Thank you, Miss Bella, for I surely believe!
I'll rest from my platemaking and praise God all I please!

Psalm 150:6 NIV
"Let everything that has breath praise the LORD."

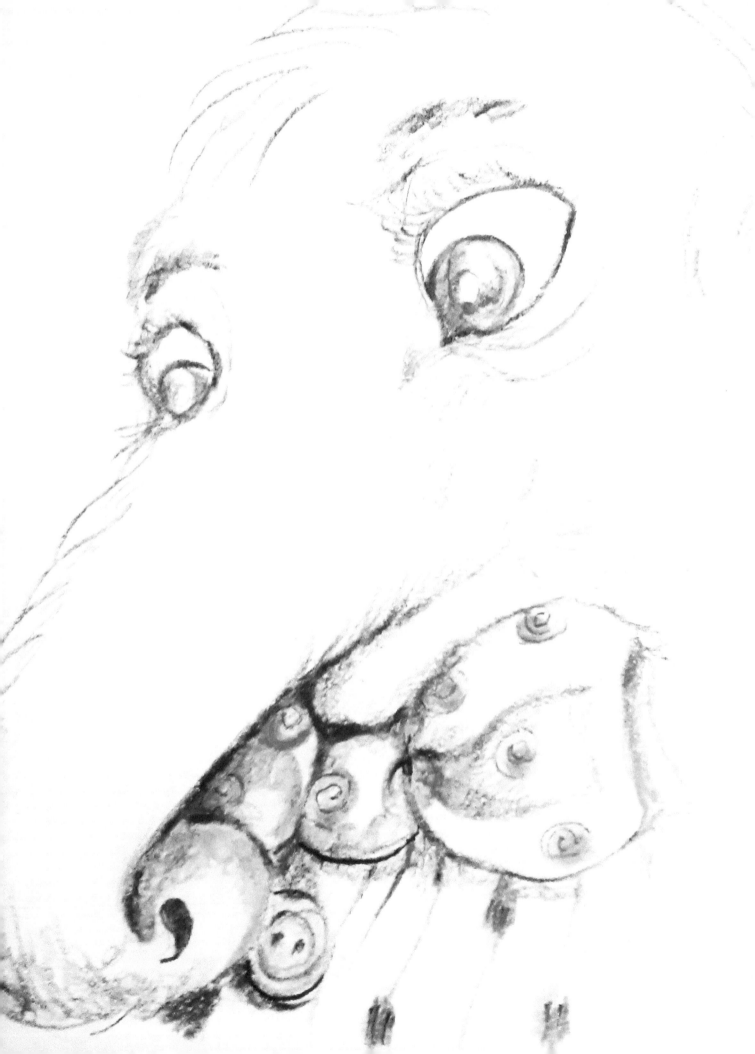

At the start beginning of the dawning of the very next day,
Wiggle McFiggle remembered his promise of not forgetting to pray,
Uplifted, again he sang praises to God,
This day would be better with no intention to plod.

Psalm 90:14 NIV
Satisfy us in the morning with your unfailing love,
that we may sing for joy and be glad all our days.

On his way out, not forgetting his shout,
Hallelujah to God! From outside his house,
His neighbors now poised, and the town all about,
Heard Mr. McFiggle again, their hearts he did rouse.
No other day did he give them dismay,
Wiggle McFiggle remembering his part,
To focus on God so He'd stay in his heart!

Psalm 119:10 KJV
With my whole heart have I sought thee:
O let me not wander from thy commandments.

CPSIA information can be obtained
at www.ICGtesting.com
Printed in the USA
LVHW072221010621
689027LV00001B/90